GILBERT THE GREAT

Martin, forever in our hearts.
J.C.
For Chris, with thanks.
C.F.

The great white shark is one of the supreme predators of the ocean. White sharks can grow to about
6 meters, the females being a little bigger than the males, and can weigh over 3 tons. But, in spite of their size,
white sharks can leap clear out of the water!

White sharks are found in parts of the Pacific, Atlantic, and Indian Oceans, and in the Mediterranean Sea.
Because of their rarity and secretive behavior, there is much we do not know about great white sharks.

In warmer waters sharks are often accompanied by a small fish called a remora. Remoras can have
a close relationship with a shark, scavenging for leftover food and nibbling off shrimp-like parasites that grow
on the shark's body. The remora may stay with a single shark for a while, hitching a lift by sticking to the shark's
underside with a special sucker found on its head.

STERLING CHILDREN'S BOOKS and the distinctive Sterling Children's Books logo are trademarks
of Sterling Publishing Co., Inc. 1166 Avenue of the Americas, New York, NY 10036

Paperback edition published in 2016.
Previously published by Sterling Publishing, Co., Inc. in a different format in 2005.
Published by arrangement with Simon & Schuster UK Ltd.

ISBN 978-1-4549-1912-4

Distributed in Canada by Sterling Publishing
c/o Canadian Manda Group, 664 Annette Street
Toronto, Ontario, Canada M6S 2C8

For information about custom editions, special sales, and premium and corporate purchases, please contact
Sterling Special Sales at 800- 805-5489 or specialsales@sterlingpublishing.com.

Manufactured in China
Lot #:
4 6 8 10 9 7 5
01/19

www.sterlingpublishing.com

GILBERT THE GREAT

by Jane Clarke
illustrated by Charles Fuge

STERLING CHILDREN'S BOOKS
New York

*F*rom the time Gilbert the great white shark was
a tiny pup, Raymond the remora stuck to him like glue.
Raymond was always at Gilbert's side.

When Gilbert was stuck in the seaweed,
Raymond untangled him.

When Gilbert got dirty, Raymond cleaned him up.

And when Gilbert lost his first row of teeth,
Raymond helped him collect them for the tooth fairy.

Gilbert and Raymond had lots of fun.
They loved to play finball, tide and seek,
and sardines. They shared everything.

Then one day Raymond told Gilbert that his family had to move across the ocean.

"I don't want to go, but Mom says I have to," cried Raymond.
As Raymond and his family swam away, Gilbert's mother hugged him tight and tried to comfort him.

"Raymond's my best friend," said Gilbert.

"Why did he have to go away? It's not fair!"

"I know," said Mom, "but his family couldn't just leave him behind."

She kissed Gilbert on the snout.
"Go and play tide and seek with the pilot fish.
It will keep your mind off Raymond."
But Gilbert couldn't stop thinking about his friend.

"I want to move with Raymond," Gilbert said.

"He's moved too far away," said Mom. "We have to stay here.
Let's go watch the basketball game. The Thrashing Threshers
are playing the Tidal Tigers. Who do you want to win?"

Gilbert looked around. There were remoras everywhere,
but none of them was Raymond.

"I don't care!" he said, and he swam off before either side scored a basket.

"It's my fault Raymond moved," Gilbert snapped as he passed an eel.
"Last week I called him a sucker!"

"You didn't make Raymond leave," Mom smiled. "Everyone fights sometimes."

The clown fish did their best to cheer Gilbert up, but nothing could make him smile.

The next day at school, everyone was very kind to Gilbert. They even gave him an extra long turn on the sea-saw.

"Cheer up," said Marvin the Mallet. "There are plenty of fish in the sea!"

"There isn't another Raymond," said Gilbert.

Gilbert was still sulking when Mom came to collect him from school.
"It's not the same without Raymond," Gilbert pouted.

That night Gilbert cried and cried and cried and his warm tears mingled with the cold ocean water.

The next morning Mom took Gilbert gently by the fin and towed him into shallow water. Rocked by the gentle waves, they gazed out at the seashore and the bright blue sky.

"I hope Raymond's new home is as nice as this," said Gilbert.

"I'm sure it is," said Mom.

"I'm hungry," Gilbert said suddenly.

"We'll go to the Wreck," said Mom.

Gilbert's eyes lit up. They didn't usually go to the Wreck.

Mom didn't like him eating junk food.

"Scrunch...Munch...Crunch."
As Gilbert was biting into a pile of
tin cans and bits of old boat, he spotted
a small remora crying in the shadows.
Gilbert stopped crunching and swam
towards her.

"What's the matter?" Gilbert asked.

"Mom and I moved and I had to leave my shark behind," she sobbed. "Now I don't have any friends."

"My remora had to move too," said Gilbert sadly. "I'm so lonely."

Gilbert and the remora looked at each other and smiled wobbly smiles.

"I'm Gilbert," said Gilbert.

"I'm Rita," replied the remora.

Just then a ray of sunlight filtered through the deep blue ocean. Gilbert's teeth flashed as he grinned a huge grin.
"Do you want to play finball with me, Rita?" he asked.

Sunlight danced in Rita's eyes.
"I'd love to," she said, and the two new friends swam off to find a ball to play with.

$\mathcal{T}$he $\mathcal{E}$nd